For Ferdinand — JE

For Elinor, my friend who loves leaves! — CJC

Text copyright © 2009 by Jonathan Emmett
Illustrations copyright © 2009 by Caroline Jayne Church

Library of Congress Cataloging-in-Publication Data
Emmett, Jonathan.
Leaf trouble / by Jonathan Emmett ; illustrated by Caroline Jayne Church.
p. cm.
Summary: A young squirrel panics when the leaves on his tree change color and fall, but he
feels better when his mother tells him about autumn.

ISBN-13: 978-0-545-16070-4
ISBN-10: 0-545-16070-7

[1. Autumn—Fiction. 2. Leaves—Fiction. 3. Squirrels—Fiction.] I.
Church, Caroline, ill. II. Title.

PZ7.E696Le 2009
[E]—dc22

2009008268

The art in *Leaf Trouble* was created dimensionally, in inks and using collage for a variety of
patterns and textures, then lit to further refine depth and perspective, and photographed.

10 9 8 7 6 5 4 3 2 1   09 10 11 12 13

Printed in China
First American edition, August 2009

Text was set in P22 Kane.
Book design by Whitney Lyle

JJ
Emmett
Jonathan

Deasmy

Leaf
Trouble

by **Jonathan Emmett**

Illustrated by
Caroline Jayne Church

Chicken House

Scholastic Inc. / New York

A fresh breeze blew across the woodland, tickling the tall grass and trembling the trees. Summer had left and autumn had arrived.

Pip Squirrel stuck his head out of the nest and sniffed the air.

"Something's changed!" he decided. And he scampered off to find out what it was.

Pip's nest was in an old oak tree.
Pip loved the old tree and he knew
every bit of it, from twig to trunk.

But something was happening to the tree.
It was happening so slowly that Pip
hadn't noticed it — until now.

He skittered to a stop and stared
at the leaves beside him.

He was so

surprised

that he

let go

of the

trunk.

"Wwwaaaahhhhh!"

squealed Pip as he tumbled down
through the branches
and landed — "OOOOOF!" —
on the woodland floor.

OOOOOF!

Pip lay there for a moment, staring up at the leaves.

"They've changed color!" he gasped.

And he was right. The last time Pip

had looked closely at the leaves,

they had all been GREEN —

but now there were lots of colors:

YELLOW and ORANGE

and even RED!

As Pip watched, one of the
leaves dropped off and

drifted

down,

toward

the

ground.

He jumped up and ran after it and
caught it in his paws.
But, even as he reached it, another
leaf began to fall.

Pip ran after the second leaf and
just managed to catch it before it
touched the woodland floor.
"Not again!" gasped Pip as a third
leaf began to fall.

Pip was still racing around, trying to catch the
falling leaves, when his sister,
Blossom, scurried up.

"Good," panted Pip. "You're just in time."

"Just in time for what?" asked Blossom.

"To help save the tree," puffed Pip.
"It's falling to pieces!"

"But that's been happening for days," said Blossom,
pointing to the leaf-covered ground.

"Then we've got to stop it NOW!"
insisted Pip.

Pip and Blossom collected all
the fallen leaves into a big pile.

"Now what?" asked Blossom.

"We put them back," said Pip.

So Blossom carried the leaves up into the tree, where Pip tried to stick them back onto the branches.

But it didn't work very well.

Then — all of a sudden — there was a HUGE
gust of wind and HUNDREDS
OF LEAVES began to fall!

Pip and Blossom were scrambling around
frantically, trying to gather them,
when Mom Squirrel arrived.

"What are you two up to?"
she asked.

When Mom found out what
Pip and Blossom had been doing,
she couldn't help smiling.

"But Pip," she said,
"the tree has to lose its leaves."

And she explained that taking care
of the leaves was hard work for the
tree and that, after keeping them all
summer, it needed to rest for a while.

"But I love this tree," said Pip sadly. "It's our home. And I want it back the way it was!"

"It will be," said Mom. "When spring comes, the leaves will all come back again. They've only gone away for a while."

"Like when the sun sets and then comes back again?" said Pip.

"Like when the sun sets," agreed Mom. "Except the leaves will take just a little longer to come back."

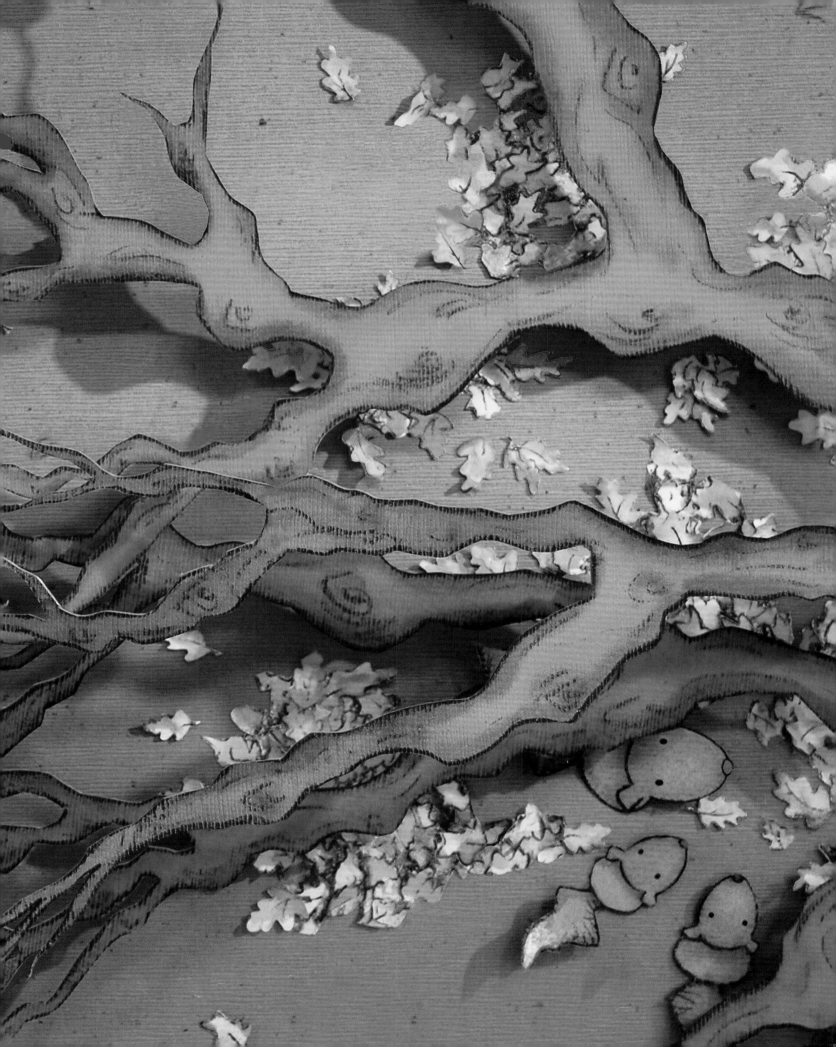

Pip, Blossom, and Mom played beneath
the old oak tree until sunset.

Before they left, they collected some leaves to take back to their nest.

"They're such beautiful colors," said Pip, smiling. "And now I understand why."

He held up a pawful of leaves to show Blossom and Mom.

"They're the colors of the sunset!" said Pip.